THOMAS ᴬᴺᴰ TOBY

W9-AHA-787

Illustrated by Tommy Stubbs

Random House 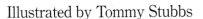 New York

Thomas the Tank Engine & Friends®

A BRITT ALLCROFT COMPANY PRODUCTION
Based on The Railway Series by The Reverend W Awdry. © 2003 Gullane (Thomas) LLC.
Thomas the Tank Engine & Friends and Thomas & Friends are trademarks of Gullane Entertainment Inc.
Thomas the Tank Engine & Friends is Reg. U.S. Pat. TM Off.

A HIT Entertainment Company

Published in the United States by Random House Children's Books, a division of Random House, Inc., New York,
and simultaneously in Canada by Random House of Canada Limited, Toronto.

www.randomhouse.com/kids/thomas   www.thomasthetankengine.com

Library of Congress Cataloging-in-Publication Data
Awdry, W. Thomas and Toby / illustrated by Tommy Stubbs. p.   cm.
"Based on The railway series by the Rev. W. Awdry."
SUMMARY: Introduces Toby the steam engine, relating how he and Henrietta came to run the quarry branch and how
he came to be friends with Thomas and the other engines.
ISBN 0-375-82593-2
[1. Railroads—Trains—Fiction. 2. England—Fiction.] I. Awdry, W. Railway series. II. Stubbs, Tommy, 1955– ill. III.
Title. PZ7.A9613Tf 2003   [E]—dc21   2003001003

Printed in the United States of America   First Edition   10 9 8 7 6 5 4 3 2 1

One sunny morning, Thomas the Tank Engine was happily chugging along his branch line. Being a Really Useful Engine, Thomas had many responsibilities, and it was important that he stayed Right on Time. Pulling Annie and Clarabel, Thomas started toward the quarry for his first delivery of the day.

Thomas was especially careful on one part of his branch
line because it ran beside a long stretch of road.
  "Peep, peep!" He'd whistle hello to anyone who might be
near, so they'd have plenty of time to get out of the way.

This late summer morning, as Thomas chugged around a bend, he noticed a policeman standing by the next crossing. Thomas had been close friends with the old constable, who'd recently retired.

This must be the new constable, thought Thomas, and he greeted the policeman with a friendly *"peep, peep."*

But the new constable's reply was far from friendly.
Thomas had startled him, and he stopped Thomas in his tracks.
"My very first day, and already there's trouble. Just who
are you and where do you think you are going?" asked the
red-faced policeman.

Thomas did his best to explain, but the policeman was not in a mood to listen to an engine.

"No cowcatcher? Not a single side plate in sight? You shouldn't travel near these public roads. It's too dangerous!" he exclaimed as he inspected Thomas.

"This cannot continue. I must speak with the person in charge."

Thomas told him that Sir Topham Hatt, the head of the railway, was on vacation. There was nothing Thomas could say to calm the policeman and nothing to do until Sir Topham Hatt returned.

"Troublemaker," muttered the policeman as Thomas chugged sadly away.

Sir Topham Hatt was having a much better time than Thomas. He was vacationing with his family on the other side of Sodor. His grandchildren had discovered an old-fashioned steam tram that still gave rides to passengers.

The short and sturdy tram's name was Toby. He had cowcatchers, side plates, and a cheery bell that he rang to greet all he met. He traveled with Henrietta, a tram coach whom he considered a good, if sometimes fussy, friend.

Long ago, they were very busy transporting goods and people to the Main Line. But now almost everyone traveled by cars and buses. Toby and Henrietta spent their days giving tram rides to people on vacation.

Being the kind of family who enjoyed railways, the Hatts returned to Toby every day of their vacation for a ride. It didn't take long for Toby to recognize that Sir Topham Hatt was a special passenger. He asked all the right questions and knew just about everything there was to know about trains and trams.

"What is your name?" asked Sir Topham Hatt as the Hatts took the last tram ride of their vacation.

"Toby, sir."

"Thank you, Toby, for a very memorable vacation."

"Thank you, sir," said Toby politely. Toby thought to himself, This gentleman is a gentleman who knows how to speak to engines.

Sadly, a few days later, Toby and Henrietta's line was shut down and they were sent to their sheds.

When Sir Topham Hatt returned from vacation, he was informed immediately about Thomas' trouble with the new constable.

He remembered Toby. He knew that underneath the chipped paint and rusty spots was a very useful tram engine who could handle the quarry line . . . *and* the prickly policeman. And there were plenty of other things to keep Thomas occupied as well.

Soon Toby and Henrietta arrived and they took to their new jobs very quickly. Toby was especially good at making the trucks behave. Thomas noticed this right away and was very impressed. He knew firsthand how troublesome those trucks could be. In no time, Thomas and Toby became good friends.

James, however, was not at all impressed with Toby. He often met Toby and Henrietta at the junction. Every time he saw them, he made a crack about how dirty they were or how slow they moved.

One day, Toby had had enough. "*Whoosh*," Toby cried, blowing out a great burst of steam. "Why must you always be so mean?"

"Oh bother," replied James. "I don't have time right now for dirty, slow engines like you. Really splendid, fast engines like myself have lots to do." Off he sped to his next stop, leaving Toby in a cloud of steam.

James continued on his route, picking up more and more trucks. He was still a bit cranky and very distracted. As he was traveling down Gordon's Hill, James was so busy thinking of things to say to Toby that he forgot to pin down his brakes. Faster, faster he flew as the trucks bumped and pushed him down the steep hill, for they loved to go fast and make trouble.

"I've got to stop," screeched James as he pulled on the brakes.

But it was no use. James could not slow down.

"Hurray," cheered the trucks . . . and then . . .

Crash!

James had finally stopped at the bottom of the hill. He'd run straight into two tar wagons.

What a sticky, dirty mess!

A short time later, the breakdown train and all available engines arrived to help with the cleanup. Toby immediately started getting the trucks under control.

When he saw James, Toby couldn't resist having a little fun.

"Is that *James*?" Toby asked innocently. "It can't be. James is such a splendid, fast engine."

James pretended he didn't hear Toby. And from that day on, James was a lot nicer.

Toby knew just about everything when it came to moving trucks. He had many years of experience and a very patient nature. So Sir Topham Hatt asked Toby to coach Mavis, a new diesel engine at the Ffarquhar Quarry.

Like most new engines, especially diesels, Mavis thought she knew it all, or at least more than that old-fashioned tram did! She quickly grew bored with moving the trucks at the quarry. More than anything, she wanted to be on the line.

One wet but very busy day, Toby asked Mavis to bring the trucks
to the line. Mavis was thrilled.

"Take it slow," he warned.

"Watch the wet rails," he suggested.

"Keep an eye on the trucks," he reminded.

But Mavis was too excited to pay attention to Toby.

As soon as she started on her way, though, she wished she'd listened more closely. The trucks realized she was new at this. The cold autumn rain made the rails extra slick, so they bumped and pushed, and before she knew it, Mavis was stalled right in the middle of a busy crossing.

Soon there were many angry people who needed to get by. Mavis didn't know what to do, and the trucks just laughed at her. She knew that Toby would be angry.

And he was. But Toby also remembered that it was Mavis' first time on the line and how tricky those trucks could be. He helped Mavis out of the crossing and promised to spend more time teaching her at the quarry.

Toby had been there only a short while, but already his hard work was recognized. Sir Topham Hatt gave both him and Henrietta a long-overdue fresh coat of paint and some shiny new parts. And best of all, Toby got a new number of his own. Now he, too, truly was a Really Useful Engine.

Toby and Thomas' friendship grew and grew. Thomas especially liked it when he found out that Toby always startled the not-so-cheery policeman with a cheery ring of his bell!